ARCADE OR BUST!

ARCADE OR BUST!

BY AMARIS GLASS

Random House 🏠 New York

"Lincoln, can you hold Hops while I clean out his cage?"

"Lincoln, I need you to teach me how to Hula-Hoop."

"Lincoln, will you help me polish my coffins?"

Sisters. They all want a piece of you.

Picture this: I'm Lincoln Loud, minding

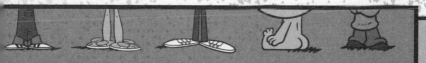

my own business in my linen-closet-turned-bedroom, doing a little dance in my undies because it's Saturday.

But not just any old regular no-big-deal-nothing-to-do Saturday. Today was the most exciting Saturday in the history of weekends! I had freedom (my parents were away all day at a seminar on singing to your houseplants to help them grow). I had quarters (Captain Coinbottom, my piggybank, was practically too heavy to carry). And I had a quest: be the first in line with Clyde at the arcade to play *Marshmallow Martian Blasters.*

What's *Marshmallow Martian Blasters,* you ask? It's only the most legendary, full-size, never-been-played-before video game known to kid-kind. It was one of the first games to appear in arcades when our parents were in grade school. *No kid living* has ever seen it in real life. Like Bigfoot.

Only, we've managed to find it!

And it's coming to Gus's Games and Grub.

"Lincoln!" Luna pounded on my door, interrupting my undies dance. "Project Day meeting in five minutes!"

No.

NO.

Nooooooo.

Not Project Day. Not today!

I flopped down on my bed and groaned into my pillow. This ruined *everything*. Why did Lori have to invent this miserable tradition, anyway?

Project Day is just what it sounds like: a day

full of projects. In a house with eleven kids, two parents, four pets, and one Vanzilla, someone is always trying to get something done. Usually several someones, and they all need help.

I admit, Project Day can be pretty handy when you want to build a bike ramp in the backyard but can't do it by yourself. In a family this size, there's always someone with the skills you need to get your project done. Everyone helps everyone, knowing that the next time Project Day rolls around, the favor will be returned.

Like I said, it's not a bad deal—unless you already have plans. *Big* plans. Important plans. Intergalactically pivotal plans! Why todaaaayyyyy? *Whyyyyyyyy?*

"Lincoln—er, Firesticks! Are you there?

Come in, Firesticks!" Clyde's voice crackled from my walkie-talkie. "Are you ready for Operation Be First in Line to Play *Marshmallow Martian Blasters* and Get the High Score? Over."

I stretched my leg out and grabbed the walkie with my toes—a skill I spent one very bored week last summer perfecting while all my sisters were sick—and pressed the button to talk to Clyde.

"I'm here, but I have bad news, buddy." I took a deep breath. "Lori's decided—"

"That she's done with old Too-Tall McSkinnyPants and is in the market for someone new?" I could practically hear Clyde smoothing his hair.

"*Clyde!* Focus! It's bad." I slid down to the

floor. "She's instituting Project Day. Today."

"No."

"Yes."

"*No.*"

"*Yes.*"

"Lincoln, this ruins *everything*!"

"I know! What am I going to do?"

More pounding on my door, this time from Lola. "You better be getting dressed, Lincoln. No one wants to see you in your underwear!"

"Clyde, they're coming for me. How do I get out of this?" I jumped up and began stuffing my backpack with clothes, comics, and my secret stash of fruit leather. The situation was dire. I might have to run away.

"Lincoln, this is bad. Over."

"I know."

"Like, *really* bad. Over. Project Days can last forever! Over."

"I *know*! Clyde, you're not helping. Over."

"Sorry. Okay, let's just take a minute to breathe. . . ." I could hear Clyde inhaling and exhaling so deep *I* was getting dizzy. "Of course! We need an Operation."

Right. "A *new* Operation," I said.

"A Get Out of Project Day Operation."

"A Get Out of Project Day Without Making Everyone Mad Operation."

"A Divert and Distract Escape Operation?" asked Clyde.

I considered it. That had worked well for me in the past, but . . . "No, I think more of a Fool My Sisters and Then Walk Merrily Away Operation."

"Ah, a Help with Project Day Without Actually Helping Operation. Classic."

"A Be Really Eager but Absolutely Useless So No One Will Want My Help and I Can Sneak Away Without Anyone Knowing What I'm Really Up To Operation."

"Lincoln, that's genius!"

It really was. "And I haven't even gotten to the best part. Every Project Day has a Floater, and if I can convince everyone to pick me, I won't be tied to one certain project. I'll float around, and no one will know where I'm supposed to be. When I disappear, no one will even know I'm gone. Poof!"

"Whoa . . . you're an inspiration. I'm proud to call you my best friend."

"Thanks, Clyde. Me too." Part of me knew

that didn't even make sense, but I was so impressed with myself I let it slide and did a somersault off the bed, landing in a gloriously awkward heap that did nothing to dampen my enthusiasm. "This is totally going to work. *Marshmallow Martian Blasters,* here we come!"

Lori and Leni's room was full of sisters and chatter as I raced inside and hurled myself onto Leni's bed. "Hey, guys! Happy Project Day!"

Everyone stopped and stared at me. Lola reached over and touched my forehead. "Do you have a fever? Why are you being weird?"

I batted her hand away and grinned at

everyone. "Who's being weird? I'm just excited!"

Lori sighed. "Whatever, Lincoln. We have a busy day ahead of us, so let's get started."

Everyone shrugged and went back to what they were doing. Except Lucy. She was still watching me.

Or maybe she wasn't. It was hard to tell under all those bangs. I pretended to pick my nose, just to see if she was watching me or not.

Lucy made a face. "Gross, Lincoln."

Whoops. Guess she was.

Lori pounded her shoe on the dresser like a judge with a gavel. "Project Day meeting will now come to order. First order of business: The Listing of the Projects. Coin toss to decide which sequence we go in." She pointed her shoe around the room. "Who has a coin?"

I hastily fished a quarter out of my pocket—courtesy of Captain Coinbottom's bottom—and tossed it to her. "Here, it's on me."

Lori caught the quarter and looked at it, then over at me. "Thanks. Wait, are you sure you're not up to something? You're being awfully helpful."

"That's because I'm a helpful guy!"

Lori rolled her eyes and flipped the quarter in the air. "Leni, call it for the older siblings," she said. Then she caught the coin and slapped it onto the back of her hand without looking.

"Call it what?" Leni asked. "Does it have a name? Lincoln, do you name your quarters? You're so smart!"

"No, Leni." Lori groaned. "Call it for the coin toss. Heads or tails."

"But what *kind* of tails? Ponytails or pigtails? They're both such cute hairstyles!"

"Just forget it, Leni. Lisa, you call it for the younger siblings."

Lisa immediately started scribbling on the whiteboard. "Though the probability of getting either heads or tails would seem to be fifty/fifty based on the one-to-one ratio, statistics show that the coin has one hundred thousandth of a percent higher chance of—"

"Just call it!" we all chorused. Lisa could keep us here all day talking about ratios.

She sighed and turned away from the board. "You realize that asking me to call it—heads, for the record—is akin to rigging the toss." She reached over to Lori and peeled back the hand covering the quarter. "One hundred thousandth of a percent. *Heads*."

Lori held up the coin so we could all see. "She's right. Heads. Younger siblings first."

Lynn, Luan, Luna, and Leni all groaned. Now they had to help with the younger kids' projects first before they could do their own. Normally, as the exact middle child, I could fall into either camp, since with eleven kids, someone's always left over.

But today was not a normal day.

Lori leaned over and picked up Lily, handing her the marker. "Okay, Lily, what project do you want to work on today?"

Lily cooed and scribbled next to the number one on the whiteboard, then dropped the marker and blew a raspberry at all of us. Lori gave her a squeeze and then set her down so we could all see her scribbles.

"It's a . . . cow. No, a beret," guessed Leni.

"Looks more like flowers," Lana said, squinting. "Ones that have been mown down, though."

"Maybe she wants to decorate her crib in the darker colors of the soul, like black and purple," offered Lucy. "Her crib is so . . . white."

Lori sighed. "She obviously wants to grab some toys and head outside to get some sun. As oldest, I have first dibs on which project I will assist, so I'm choosing to help Lily."

The others groaned, but those are the rules. Lily, as the youngest, gets first project, and Lori, as the oldest, gets First Helper rights.

"Lisa, you're next." Lori handed the marker to Lisa, who hopped up on the stool and—

no surprise—started writing what turned out to be a *very* long sentence, full of numbers, letters, and some symbols I didn't recognize. I managed to decipher the words *melanin* and *oxybenzone* before giving up and mentally running through some of the maneuvers for outwitting the sentient Licorice Lassos who defend the Chocolate Fountain Fortress.

"Well?" Lisa dropped the marker and turned around. "Whose skills are best suited to my project's needs?" She tapped her foot on top of the stool.

I raised my hand. "Uh, Lisa . . . no one knows what that says."

She sighed and rubbed her forehead. "It says—oh, never mind. I'll take a test subject instead. I need a certain amount of melanin. . . ."

Leni raised her hand. "Ooooh, I love

melons! My favorite is cantaloupe."

"No, Leni, *melanin*, not—" Lisa sighed. "Never mind. I suppose you'll do."

"Great! Moving on." Lori took the marker from Lisa and wrote *Leni* under Lisa's science babble, then the number three with Lola's name next to it. "Lola, you're next. What's your project?"

Lola jumped up to the stool, but when her first sentence included the words *pageant* and *dancing,* I stopped listening. My brilliant plan would save me from any long-term involvement with either.

I grinned, getting lost in another daydream as my fingers twitched around an imaginary joystick. Puffy Martians surrounded me, but I fought back, purple candy lasers slicing through their sticky masses—

"Lincoln!" Lori's voice penetrated my marshmallow-filled haze.

Without thinking I blurted, "Ready the taffy torpedoes!" But there were no Martians coming at me, just a roomful of impatient and suspicious sisters.

Way scarier.

"Uhh, what are you babbling about?" Lori asked.

"Taffy torpedoes?" Lucy was too observant this morning.

Think fast, Firesticks. "Yeah, in case anyone wants to make some candy as one of their projects. Candy project, amiright?" I whooped and looked around the room for agreement, but I was greeted only by blank stares.

"Whatever, Lincoln," Lori said. "Do you

have a project or not?" Apparently they'd gone through Lana and Lucy while I'd zoned out. Lori tapped the marker against the whiteboard and waited for me to answer.

"Nope!" That came out sounding a little forced, even to my ears. I coughed and tried to sound casual. "I'm here to help all of *you*."

"Help all of *us*? What are you talking about?" Lori frowned.

I got to my feet. "Lori—excuse me, everyone—I would like to be Floater."

Lynn snort-laughed. "*You*, Floater? Yeah, right. You've got to be kidding."

"No, seriously, you guys. I'm ready. I can do it! I've been watching lots of DIY videos. Give me a chance."

"Wait a minute." Lola stuck her face right

up to mine, her eyes narrowed. "You don't have a project? Nothing you've been working toward for *weeks*?"

"Nothing you want to do today more than *anything*?" Lori chimed in.

"No secret rendezvous with Clyde?" Luna added.

"Nothing, guys," I said, forcing a laugh. "I just want to make this the best Project Day ever." I spread my arms. "I swear."

Lori shrugged. "Fine, but don't blow it." She scribbled *Floater* next to my name and motioned to Lynn, the next oldest after me. "Your turn."

I couldn't stop the huge grin that spread across my face. My plan had worked! I could float around until I had the chance to disappear.

Sisters and Marshmallow Martians, look out. I just leveled up!

Finally all the projects had been planned, and the meeting ended. I wasted no time dashing to my room to let Clyde know the good news. I grabbed the walkie from my dresser and leapt onto my bed. "Puffmaster, come in! I have awesome news to report. Over."

Static crackled through the walkie; then

Clyde came on. "Sorry, I was just filling out job applications in Tasmania for Bobby. Say that again? Over."

I did some bed dancing as I said gleefully, "I'm Project Day Floater, Clyde! Operation Convince My Sisters I'm Ready for the Responsibility went off without a hitch."

"They elected you Floater?"

"They elected me Floater! No one project can tie me down, and once I make the rounds, being worse than useless until they don't want my help anymore, I can disappear." I celebrated my extreme cleverness with a giant bounce and somersault onto the floor.

"But, Lincoln, *should* you disappear?" Clyde asked. "What if one of your sisters really needs your help?"

I kicked my feet up against my desk. "Relax,

Clyde, the projects are all pretty simple today. Besides, what about *my* project, which I've been planning for weeks?"

"I can't argue with that logic," Clyde agreed.

"Okay, now I need to implement Phase One of Operation Float Through Project Day Being Utterly Useless So No One Will Miss Me and Get to the Arcade First and Also Think of a Shorter Name for This Operation. Let me know when you arrive. Over."

"Roger that, Firesticks. Over."

I hugged Captain Coinbottom to my chest and gleefully tried to guess how many games he carried inside him. He was so heavy he dented my ribs, so I figured *hours* of blasting Martians were in my future.

But first, I needed to be the fastest and worst Floater in the history of Project Day.

The hallway was quiet as I slipped out of my room, Captain Coinbottom under my arm. When my escape moment came, I was going to be ready.

Everyone's doors were shut, so I cocked my head, listening and considering. Right now I was at about Level Ash. Starting slow. Who would be the first Sister Martian I'd goo into oblivion?

Leni's high-pitched squeals came from Lisa's room. What kind of test was Lisa subjecting her to? I frowned and avoided Lisa's door.

Luna's guitar screeched from Lana and Lola's room, so they were fine for now, too. Lily chose that moment to wander through the open bathroom door, her diaper so full it practically dragged on the floor. The smell hit me like a blast from a Moss-Muffin Moat, so bad I forgot about the Operation and was halfway back to my room when Lori stepped out of the bathroom and spotted me.

"Floater, I need your help!"

Here we go. I turned around and saluted. "At your service."

She ignored me and pointed at Lily. "Lily's

25

diaper is overdue for a change. I'd do it, but I have to shave my legs before we go outside for Lily's Hanging Out in the Sun project, so make yourself useful." She tossed me some wipes and a diaper and disappeared back inside the bathroom.

"Gladly," I called after her with a grin. I leaned over and picked up Lily, holding my breath. This Operation was off to a stinky start.

"Poo-poo," said Lily, and blew a raspberry against my cheek.

"Exactly." Wiping the spit from my face, I peeked through the open bathroom door. Lori sat perched on the edge of the tub in shorts and a bikini top, her back to me. Good.

Holding my finger to my lips, I stepped inside and carefully laid Lily down on the rug. I don't know if she understood me or not, but she didn't make a sound as I peeled off her overfull diaper and slid it away from us, closer to Lori.

Cleaning Lily up and breathing through my mouth, I kept an eye on Lori, waiting for her reaction.

Three, two, one . . .

Lori's head snapped up and she paused, her razor in the air. I heard her sniff, and then—

"Ugh, what is that *smell*?" She looked over her shoulder and spotted the diaper. "Gah! What is that doing— *Lincoln!*" Lori leapt into the tub and glowered at me. "What are you doing in here? And why isn't *that*"— she pointed at the diaper with one hand and plugged her nose with the other—"in the trash can *IN LILY'S ROOM*?"

I pasted a bewildered expression on my

face. "What's wrong with the bathroom? I've changed her diaper in here before. I've changed her diaper in every room in the house!"

"What's wrong is that I can't breathe!" Lori leaned out of the tub and wrenched open the bathroom window.

"But this way is more efficient. I can clean her up and immediately toss the flushable wipe into the toilet." I demonstrated as I spoke, and flushed with flourish. "Voilà! No more wipe, no more stink."

"Lincoln, there is *definitely* a stink! Will you please just give Lily to me and get that diaper *out of here*!"

"You bet!" I passed Lily off to Lori with a smile that she didn't return. In fact, she glared at me as I carefully wrapped up the stinky diaper—trying not to make a face; it really was foul—and washed my hands. "Can't be too careful!" I gave her a cheerful wave and scurried out of the bathroom with the diaper and Captain Coinbottom.

Two sisters down, eight to go. Smiling to myself, I headed for the stairs. This was going to be fun.

"Lincoln!"

Ah. Sister number three.

"I mean, Floater! I need your help." Lola stood behind me in the hallway, holding a pair of high-heeled shoes.

Help? Sure. But before I could answer, Lana popped out from behind her.

"Hey, Lincoln, there you are. Hops adopted a bunch of tadpoles and I need your help naming them."

I cocked my head at her. "Hops . . . *adopted* tadpoles?"

Lana shrugged. "They belong to my class. I'm taking care of them for the weekend. And Hops has always wanted to be a dad, so . . ."

Lola dangled the heels in Lana's face. "I asked him first, and mine's important."

So is mine.

"But Hops is all confused because none of his babies have names yet," Lana said, batting at the shoes.

Lola ignored her and grabbed my hand. "I need a partner to practice the dance portion of my pageant routine."

Lana grabbed my other hand and I became

the rope in a game of sisterly tug-of-war.

"Guys, relax." *Yank left.* "There's plenty of Floater to go around—" *Yank right.* "Ow!"

"Fine," said Lola.

"Whatever," Lana huffed.

They both let go at the same time and I stumbled back, trying to keep my balance. Lola tossed the heels at me. "Put these on and look alive, Floater!"

I grabbed the shoes and followed my sisters into their room. "Um, why do I need to wear high heels?"

"Because the Tiny Dancers pageant is in a week, and the boy I'll be dancing with is taller than you," Lola said, as if the answer were super obvious. "I need to practice my smile at that neck angle."

Typical Lola. Pageant business was a topic

I usually ran from, but today I was a helpful Floater. If Lola wanted me to dance, well, I'd show her my best and most enthusiastic moves. I slapped a smile on my face and slipped off my sneakers. "Whatever you say."

I had the first shoe barely buckled when Lana yanked me over to a fishbowl crowded with squiggly little tadpoles. "Look at 'em, Lincoln. Aren't they beautiful?"

They looked like slimy, swimming boogers to me, but sure. "You bet!"

"So what about that guy? Does he look like a Poppy, do you think? Maybe a Tag? Or a Finny? Names are really important in determining a tadpole's future life as a frog. They need fun, bouncy names. Nothing too heavy or fancy. Frogs aren't uppity, like some animals."

"Uppity?"

"You know, owls and Siamese cats and Portuguese men-of-war."

"Okay, I think I get it." I pointed at one little squiggly guy. "Percival," I said with conviction. It was important to be decisive in naming tadpoles.

The look Lana gave me was pure confusion.

"Or Chauncey," I said, a name which was decisively terrible.

"*Chauncey?* Lincoln, that's an *owl* name. Weren't you listening?" Lana looked as if she wanted to take my temperature. I tried hard not to appear too satisfied. No way would she want me to help name all of them.

"Lincoln, I'm ready!" Lola grabbed my hand and dragged me to the middle of the room while I fumbled to get the other shoe on.

"Ready the accompaniment!" she bellowed.

Luna was hunkered down in the corner in front of her keyboard, a glum look on her face. As Lola's helper, she had to supply the dance music—and I was betting it wasn't British punk rock.

"Hit it," Lola said, waving her hand like a conductor.

Luna sighed and began playing what sounded like a jazzy waltz.

Lola swung me around like I was a bag of flour, my death grip on Captain Coinbottom knocking me off balance.

"Wait, I'm not even"—one of the heels went flying across the room, right into a shelf full of stuffed animals—"strapped in yet," I finished as an avalanche of unicorns, flying bison, and three-headed snowmen came tumbling down . . . right on Luna's head. She let loose a magnificent screech as she tried to extricate herself.

Lola snapped her fingers. "Lincoln, you're embarrassing yourself. Get it together!"

"Sorry." I tried to sound sheepish, but I wasn't sorry at all. "Walking in heels is hard. How do you not fall over?"

"I don't fall over because I practice." Her face was red as she scrambled to find the heel in the mess of stuffed animals. After a few seconds, she stood and stomped her foot. "And because I am *graceful*!"

"Uh . . . okay."

She shoved the heel onto my foot and buckled it too tight, but I swallowed a wince. *Focus on the Operation.*

"There! Try to keep up." Lola began spinning me around the room again, and I took the opportunity to toss another few brilliant names out to Lana. "Reginald! Spencer! Orpheus!"

I was seriously good at this.

Lana rolled her eyes. "Those are terrible names. You don't understand frogs at *all*."

"Terrence!"

"Lincoln, pay attention," Lola snapped. "We're coming up to the most important part."

Luna pounded out a very dramatic tempo that had Lola spinning me around and around, making me dizzy. She yanked my arm around her back. "The finale! You have to dip me!" she cried, throwing herself so hard she slipped out of my arms. Her heel caught on mine, and that was when I knew I was a goner. I waved my arms like a windmill before tipping over and crashing on top of her, with Luna banging the keys in a terrific, non-waltzy crescendo.

It was an epic fail.

Yes!

Lola groaned and pushed me off of her. "Your dancing is *atrocious.* Are you *trying* to ruin my life?"

I rolled over and got shakily to my feet. "Sorry. Go again?"

"Are you *crazy?* I can't risk a sprained ankle or a broken toe. Get out of here, Floater!"

I shrugged and turned to Lana. "Harold?"

"You can't name a tadpole *Harold.* Your names are worse than Lynn's, and she wanted to name them after her favorite wrestlers! Just forget it. I'll do it myself."

I saluted them both. "It has been a pleasure

serving you as Project Day Floater. My duty here is done."

Three more sisters down!

Slipping my feet out of the heels, I headed for the stairs, whistling the theme song to *Marshmallow Martian Blasters*.

There were no sisters in sight as I started down the stairs, but this is the Loud house. No sisters in sight doesn't last very long.

Right on cue, Lucy appeared at the bottom of the stairs—just as I heard Lisa's voice above me. "Floater! I am in need of your services."

Lucy waved. "So am I. And I was here first."

Lisa took a deep breath, no doubt preparing to launch into a long-winded speech, full of all the reasons her project was more important than Lucy's and therefore needed my help more.

But helping Lisa could mean being trapped all day. One time, I was her guinea pig for a super-strength cough medicine. I took one dose in the morning and woke up at eight o'clock that night in my bathrobe, missing an eyebrow.

Not today.

I set Captain Coinbottom down and held up my arms. "Guys, guys, no need to fight. There's a way to decide who gets me first. Fairly."

Lucy crossed her arms. "Life isn't fair. It's all darkness and catacombs and unrequited love."

"Well, this is Project Day, not life. And

this little game should only take seven to ten minutes, depending how quickly you guys catch on."

Lisa sighed. "Lincoln, is this really the best use of your time as Floater?"

It is when I know you'll get so frustrated by how little sense this game makes that you'll just give up and go away.

"Trust me, you're gonna love it," I said.

Lisa sighed. "Fine."

Deeper sigh. "If you insist," said Lucy.

"Okay. This is how it goes: I'll say a word, and you have to guess the word the first word makes me think of. The sister who guesses right gets to move one step closer, and the first sister to reach me gets the help of the Floater. But if you guess wrong, you have to go back a step—or maybe even go all the way back to the beginning, if you're *really* wrong. Got it?"

Lucy cocked her head at me. "What?"

Lisa's patience was already wearing thin. "I don't understand the purpose of this endeavor—"

"Flabbergast!" I cut her off with a terrific yell.

"Wait—" Lisa said, clutching her head. "I have to think—"

"Spiderweb!" Lucy said.

I pointed at Lucy. "Yes! Advance one step."

To Lisa, I said, "Sorry, *wait* is nowhere near correct."

"How is this a game?" Lisa asked, pushing her glasses up on her nose indignantly.

"No one likes a sore loser! Next word: *curtain.*"

"Deciduous!" Lisa chimed in before Lucy

could answer. Now who believed in the gaminess of this game?

"Lament," Lucy said faintly, but I was already applauding Lisa.

"Deciduous is worth *two* steps. Come on down!"

Lisa smoothed her hair and took two steps. "I simply followed the logical thought train from curtain to window to branch to—"

"Barnacle!" I hollered. Never leave them time to think logically.

"Levitation!" Lucy was ready this round, but I couldn't let her get too close.

I fake-flinched. "Ooooh, sorry, *levitation* is a forbidden word. You'll have to go back to the bottom of the stairs."

"Yes! I'm in the lead!" Lisa crowed. "I can

win games even when they don't make sense!"

"Next word: *topography*," I said.

"*Guava!*" Lucy cried, desperate.

"*Iatrogenesis!*" Lisa yelled.

Iatro-what? "Lisa, you're on top of your game today. One step for the girl with the glasses!"

Lucy raised her hand. "Lincoln, I really just need your help to—"

"*Trampoline!*" I cried. I couldn't let her finish that thought.

Startled, Lucy recovered and piped up quickly. "*Centaur!* A majestic centaur of sadness!"

Lisa, not to be outdone, shouted, "*Abdominal cavity.* A gruesome one."

I nodded, impressed. "Tie! Both of you, one step forward. Next word: *Crimea.*"

Lisa, who was one step away, almost quivered with excitement as she fumbled for a word.

But Lucy beat her to it. *"Pincushion!"*

"Pincushion, yes!" *Pincushion?* The pressure was getting to the poor girl. "That *perfect* answer is worth two steps forward, *and* your opponent has to go back to the top of the stairs."

Lisa folded her arms. "How long do we have to do this?"

"Just until one of you reaches me. It's the only *fair* way to decide who I'll help."

"Egalitarian considerations aside, my work is too important for these trifles," Lisa said. "I'll carry on without the help of the Floater."

I shrugged. "Have it your own—er— egalitarian way. Good luck to you!"

She shuffled off toward her room. I waved

and turned back to Lucy just as my walkie crackled.

"Firesticks, I'm on my way. How goes the Operation? Over." Clyde was *way* too loud. I hurried to turn down the volume, but I knew Lucy had heard him.

I offered my most helpful Floater smile. "So, your turn, Luce. How can I be of service?"

Lucy stared at the ground, her cheeks pink. "I need advice. And you're a boy."

A faint hum came from the walkie and I knew Clyde was trying to talk to me. I had to keep this moving along. "Yep, I'm a boy. Have been all my life. What's up?"

She sighed and dropped onto the bottom step. "It's Edwin. I think he's mad at me."

Uhhh . . .

Edwin was Lucy's vampire boyfriend.

Edwin was also an inanimate object.

"Um, Lucy . . . Edwin sits on a shelf and stares into space all day. There's no earthly reason for him to be mad at you."

"But lately he's been—"

"Look, just buy him a present or something, okay? Something spooky. He'll love it."

With that I grabbed the Captain and took a flying leap over the bottom step—over Lucy's head—and skidded around the corner into the dining room. The jingle of coins had me grinning from ear to ear. *Soon!*

I held the walkie close to my mouth and whispered, "It's working like a dream, Clyde. More than halfway through. Over."

"Fantastic! I'll be there soon. Over."

Seven Sister Martians down!

Bathroom: done. Bedroom: conquered. Stairs: vanquished. Now on to the first floor and the older siblings' projects.

I'd barely stepped into the kitchen before Lynn demanded my help. She stood by the table, holding the phone to her ear, and waved at me.

"Floater, can you come help me for a sec?"

I ambled over with a grin on my face. "Sure. What do you need, older sister?"

"I'm trying to win this awesome contest," she explained, with one hand over the mouthpiece. "The prize is tickets to the Royal Woods Pro Wrestling Tournament."

"Thrilling! How can I be of service?"

She shoved the phone at me. "Just listen.

I'm on hold with the radio station, but Nature is calling, and she does *not* like getting a busy signal. Keep listening. If someone comes on and asks you which wrestler famously clotheslined Alzbeta Wisniewski on top of Mount Kilimanjaro on September twenty-second, nineteen forty-eight, all you have to do is give the right answer and tell them my name."

"Oh, easy." *Too* easy. Lynn's—er—conversations with "Nature" tended to be long. No way was I going to wait here until she finished. I'd just have to convince her she didn't really want me to.

I waited until she got to the bottom of the stairs before calling after her, "What's the right answer, again?"

"Lincoln!" she said, frustrated. "It's Daphne

Alderon Zheng, Mama Zheng, Portland's portliest pile driver! *Everyone* knows that."

"Maine? Or Oregon?"

"What?"

"Portland, Maine, or Portland, Oregon? I want to get it right."

Lynn balled her fists and ground them into her cheeks. "That doesn't even matter!"

"It does to me. I don't want to mess this up for you."

"Then stop being so weird and just remember the answer!"

I grabbed a marker from the desk. "Let me just write this down. . . . Mama Wiznewski threw the other lady—Kelly—on a pile of cars in Portland?"

Lynn slapped her forehead. "Have you taken

too many hockey pucks to the brain? Why are you not listening?!"

"I am. It's just a lot of information to keep track of."

Lynn looked at what I'd written on my arm:

Eat my marshmallow puffs! Martians drool, Sergeant Puffner rules!

"Lincoln, that's not what I said at all," she said, looking at me as if I were crazy. "That's barely English."

I looked closely at my arm, then shrugged. "Strange. Could you repeat it again?"

"After such a massive brain fumble?" she asked. "No thanks. I'll just keep Nature on hold a little while longer. Clear the field!" She shooed me away, snatching the phone as if she were afraid she'd catch something.

I gave Captain Coinbottom a reassuring shake and vamoosed, heading to the back door whistling. Outside, I took a deep breath of all Saturday had to offer: sunshine, freedom, and the promise of video games.

Luan's guffaw sounded from the garage as I stepped into the yard, and I made sure to whistle louder so she'd know I was there.

It worked.

"Hey, Floater!" She stuck her head outside the garage door. "Why don't you catch that breeze and *float* over here. Get it? Hahaha!" She beckoned me over and pulled me into the garage when I got close enough. "I need your help."

I glanced around. She'd set up a little counter full of sprays, powders, and face paint. Interesting.

"What's going on in here this fine Project Day?"

Luan was wearing a color-streaked apron, and smears of paint smudged her face. Lucy sat with her back to me.

"I'm practicing my clown painting. I already did Lucy's face—"

Lucy turned around.

"Gah!" I yelled. Beneath Lucy's hair was nothing but a ghostly grin with hollow cheeks. "It looks so real."

Luan grinned proudly. "I know." Then she leaned over and whispered, "I meant to make a happy rainbow clown face. I don't know how it went so ghastly."

Lucy shrugged. "I'm allergic to rainbows." Then she nodded at me. "Hi, Lincoln."

I waved but quickly looked away. It wasn't exactly comfortable having a sad skeleton greet you by name.

I clapped my hands together. "So let's do this. What do you need?"

Luan led me to a chair facing a mirror and stood behind me. "Your head. Specifically, your hair. Lucy's is too dark to show all the colors of Mr. Sunbeam, my new clown character." With a quick glance at Lucy's fleshless face, she added, "Mr. Sunbeam is a *happy* clown."

I grinned at her reflection. "Sounds fantastic!" She'd just given me my plan: if Luan

wanted happy, then I would give her anything
but.

After trying to smooth my cowlick, Luan
grabbed a tube and squirted out a bunch of
bright green paint.

I made a concerned face. "You're starting
with green?"

"Of course! Green is the best foundation
for any good clown."

"Are you sure? Isn't it a little too . . . slimy?
As in, ghost ooze?"

Luan looked down at the green paint.
I could see the hesitation in her eyes.

I dug in deeper. "Wouldn't it be better as
an accent color? In smaller amounts it could
become candy-apple green."

Slowly Luan lowered the paint. "Maybe

you're right. . . ." She looked up at me, then back down at the paint again before setting it aside with a small shake of her head. Then she picked up a tube of purple paint and turned me around to face her. "Let's focus on the eyebrows," she said, smearing some purple on her finger and reaching for my face.

I jerked back. "Whoa, are you sure? Purple eyebrows, with my eye color? Don't you think that's a bit . . . spooky?"

She stepped back and squinted at my eyes. I opened them wide and blinked innocently. "Umm . . . I guess it *is* a little phantom-like."

I swallowed an excited smile. No way could Luan handle making *two* accidentally scary clowns in one day. She was *this close* to throwing in the towel.

She frowned and backed away, tilting her head as she studied me. Then she nodded and spun me back to face the mirror.

"I've got it!" She smiled triumphantly at me. "Gold wings over each ear. They're not scary!" She started to tug on the hair over my ears and tried to puff it out.

This time *I* tilted my head critically and studied my face. "I don't know—kind of looks like devil horns."

Her smile fell a little. "You think they look like horns?"

I held up my hands. "I could be wrong. I'm sure you know what you're doing. If you say happy clowns can have pokey devil horns, then by all means, horn away!" I leaned back and smiled at her in the mirror.

She tugged a little more on the poufs over my ears, then sighed and smoothed them down. "Thanks for your help, Floater, but it's just not working. I guess it's back to juggling tiny tricycles for this clown artiste."

"Of course, whatever you need. I'm the Floater, here to help!" I whipped off the towel she'd laid over my shoulders and hopped down from the stool.

"Bye, Corpse Lucy!" I threw her a careless wave, but her teeth-lips didn't move. She just watched me with that ghostly stare as I shrugged and left the garage.

Nine down.

One to go.

My walkie-talkie crackled. "Lincoln, I'm on my way. What's your status? Over."

I quickly ducked behind the steps. "Status is good, but do *not* come to the front door or the back door. I repeat, stay away from *all* female Louds. Project Day is still in full swing.

The Operation is still at risk. Don't let anyone see you! Let's meet at base camp. Over!"

"You mean in the bushes under the porch? In all the dirt?"

"That's what I said. Base camp! Over and out!"

Hugging Captain Coinbottom to my chest, I went around to the front of the house, making myself available for my last sister, who might—

"Lincoln!"

I smiled. *Need my help.*

I turned to the porch and bowed. "Leni! How can I— Whoa. What happened to you? Why are you . . . *blue*?"

Leni's blond hair looked brighter than usual against the deep blue of her face, which was very, very blue.

She smiled and did a spin. "Do you like

it? It's Lisa's new sunscreen. It turns your skin blue!"

"I can see that." Suddenly I was very glad I'd come up with that game to keep from having to help Lisa. I was supposed to *blast* Martians, not *become* one.

Leni bounced down the steps and over to me. "I need your help, Floater. I have a new project."

"You want me to help wash it off?"

"Wash it off? Are you kidding? I love it! I feel like a superhero or something!"

"A superhero?"

"Yes! Like those people with cat faces from that one movie, or a blueberry!" Leni said. "Look, I already made a costume." She twirled and an orange cape flared out from her shoulders. Her dress was covered in straps and buckles. Her boots came up past her knees and were painted all over with tiger stripes.

"Wow. A blueberry tiger. That's . . . something." I meant it. It was definitely something.

"Thanks! And now I need your help. What does a superhero *do*?"

"Do?"

"Yeah. Do they hang out at the mall? Do they paint one another's nails and watch videos? I feel as if I have this whole tribe of *my people* and I don't even know them."

"Um . . . okay, well, if you want to know what superheroes do, you have to read their stories."

"Great! Where do I find these stories?"

I grinned. "Comic books. Lots and lots of comic books." *That should keep her busy for*

a day or four. "You can read mine. I give you permission to enter my room and go through my stash."

Leni gave a little jump and squealed. "*All* of them?"

I nodded solemnly. "All of them. You might find something you really like."

She clapped her hands and hugged me before I could duck out of the way. Luckily, none of the blue rubbed off. "Thank you, Linky!"

"You're welcome, Superhero . . . Blueberry."

Leni beamed and bounced off. I watched her go inside, and with the click of the door I was home free. No more Floating. As soon as Clyde got here, we could head to the arcade.

Just then, in a brilliant show of perfect timing, Clyde's voice came over the walkie.

"Firesticks, I have arrived at base camp.

I repeat, I have arrived. What's your ETA? Over!"

"On my way, buddy. Over."

Home. Free.

Grinning, I checked to make sure no one was watching, then dropped to my hands and knees and crawled into the bushes.

Clyde held perfectly still, so quiet I wasn't even sure he was there, until I whistled our secret call. Then he popped out. "Lincoln! Buddy! It's finally happening!"

I pumped my fist. "I know. The day we've been working so hard for is finally here! Do you have everything?"

Clyde opened his backpack. "We've got

water for hydration in case we get sweaty gaming, bandanas to keep the sweat out of our eyes for better gaming vision, snacks for energetic sweating, batteries for our walkies in case our sweaty hands make them fry, and eleven weeks' allowance."

"This is gonna be a great day," I said, gazing out as though I could see the horizon instead of the latticework covering the bottom of the porch. "Legendary."

"We've been waiting for this day for so long." Clyde wiped away a tear of happiness.

I grabbed him by the shoulders. "Keep it together, Clyde. We still have to get there. Are you ready? Where'd you park your tandem bike?"

"It's in the bushes on the side of the yard. Everything's ready to go, Linc—"

Just then, our walkies crackled.

Clyde looked at me. I looked at him.

"But . . ." I pointed at Clyde. "You're here." I pointed at myself. "And I'm here." I looked around the barren space under the porch. "Who could it be? We're both here."

The walkie crackled again. Clyde and I grabbed each other. "They're haunted!"

Before we had time to be embarrassed about our manly show of fear, a voice came through. "Clyde? Are you there?" A *grown-up* voice.

Oh no.

"I'm sorry, Clyde. I know I'm never supposed to use this to talk to you when you're with Lincoln, but this is an emergency."

No.

I grabbed Clyde's arm. "Your *dad*? Clyde,

no adults on this frequency! We swore a blood oath!"

Clyde hung his head, ashamed. "I know, Lincoln. I'm sorry! They promised they'd only use it for emergencies . . . and for playing *Hide-and-Sing*."

"Hide and *what*? Never mind, just—"

"Clyde, are you there? How do you use this thing?" Clyde's dad must have fumbled with the controls, because a piercing screech came from the walkies. Clyde and I both covered our ears.

"Sorry! Clyde, I repeat, come home."

Clyde picked up his walkie. "I'm here, Dad. What's the emergency?"

"Son, I'm sorry to do this to you, but your father just found out this is the last day to qualify for the Royal Woods Geocaching Championship. We thought it was tomorrow, but now we need to find the last three caches and, well, you know we can't do it without you. We desperately need our Clydesdale."

Clyde and I looked at each other, stricken. I shook my head fiercely. *"Marshmallow Martians,"* I mouthed.

Clyde pressed the button. "Can it wait a few hours? Lincoln and I were just about to—"

"I'm sorry, son, but we might not have enough time as it stands. You know how important this is to your dad."

Clyde lifted his palms and made a *what can I do?* face at me. He sighed into the walkie. "Of course. I'll come right back."

"Thank you, son. Please tell Lincoln I'm so sorry to interrupt. I'll make it up to you boys."

Clyde shrugged at me. "Over."

"Right! Over and goodbye! I love you! How do you turn this thing off?" Clyde and I braced ourselves for another piercing blast from the walkie; then everything went quiet.

I looked at Clyde.

Clyde looked at me.

We both sighed.

"I'm sorry, buddy. Really. But when family needs help, you have to go."

His words made me feel uncomfortable—so I immediately shoved them to the back of my mind. Guilt could wait.

Clyde tossed a bandana at me. "But you can still go. Make me proud!"

I took the bandana and offered him a salute. "It shall be so."

Clyde shouldered his backpack and crawled

out from under the porch. I listened to him drag his bike from the bushes and slowly ride down the street, his wheel noisemaker squeaking out a sad song for our ruined day.

I would not give up. Clyde was right. I *had* to go. For both of us.

And for the Martians.

Clyde had taken his tandem bike, but I could still ride my own. Just as I was about to sneak out of base camp, I heard Lori's voice from the living room window.

"Guys, what do you say we call it quits on Project Day? We're all mostly done, right?"

A faint chorus of *yeah*s and *I guess so*s

answered her; then it was quiet again.

After a minute Luna piped up. "Today was kinda wack, brah."

That seemed to unleash a dam, and suddenly everyone chimed in at once.

"I finished my project, but it somehow doesn't feel . . . *complete.*"

"I *sort* of made it work."

"Project Day didn't turn out quite the way I thought. . . ."

"Has a Floater ever managed to float around to so many projects before?"

"A better question is, has a Floater ever managed to be so weird and unhelpful before?"

"Yeah, what was his deal?"

"He was being weirder than usual, that's for sure."

Ouch. I guess that's what I deserved. I *was*

being weird today. But I didn't mean to mess up *all* of Project Day.

Lori clapped her hands. "Okay, we all agree today was kind of a bust. How about a special treat? Instead of ordering pizza, what if we go to Pizza Pirates for lunch?"

A ten-person cheer went up at her words, with even Lily cooing.

I felt a pang. That sounded fun . . . but Pizza Pirates didn't have *Marshmallow Martian Blasters* and I was on a mission.

"What about Lincoln?" Leni asked.

"I saw Clyde coming over on his tandem a little while ago, and I just heard them leave. I bet they went off somewhere to talk about how weird Lincoln's being," said Luna.

"How that Floater sank!" Luan said. "Get it?"

I groaned. Everyone inside groaned.

"So it's just us girls, then." Lori clapped her hands. "Everybody in the van in five minutes!"

Pizza Pirates is right next to Gus's Games and Grub, but if I went with my sisters and then left the pizza place to go next door, they'd know I was up to something. They'd be steamed to learn that I'd lied and deliberately messed up their projects.

I couldn't hitch a ride. My bike would have to do.

I hurried to get it out of the garage before any of them made it out to Vanzilla. I'd have to take a different route to avoid being seen, but even so, I'd be there in no time. *Marshmallow Martians, get ready to be liquefied!*

My bike was chained.

My shirt was soaked with sweat.

My sisters were nowhere in sight.

Deep breaths.

I'd made it. Gus's Games and Grub. The holy grail.

I grabbed the walkie from my belt, my

hand trembling. Then I pressed the button and practically yelled, *"Clyde!"*

"Lincoln, what is it? I'm kind of in the middle—"

"She's here. Over."

"She? You mean—"

"I made it, Clyde. I can see her through the window." I touched my fingers to the glass. "And she's *beautiful."*

"Oooh, Lincoln. Tell me *everything.* Over."

"She's tall and bright. The colors on her screen are crisp, and the pixels are so, so square. She's everything we dreamed she'd be, Clyde."

Clyde sighed over the walkie. "I wish I could be there. Get the highest score for me, will you? Over."

I saluted, though of course he couldn't see me. "You got it, buddy. Over and out."

I clicked off and, armed with Captain Coinbottom, marched into the arcade to claim the top spot I'd waited so long for.

But that spot was already filled. With kids. Waiting in a line longer than any Loud house bathroom line. Longer than the months of waiting just to get to this moment. Longer than the list of all the things I didn't buy and the things I didn't do to save up my allowance for this one, magical day.

I accidentally took a step forward—those beeps and pings were *calling* to me, I swear— and a girl in cowboy boots jerked her thumb behind her.

"Back of the line's that way, pal."

"Yeah, no cutting!"

"Who does this kid think he is? We've been waiting for hours!"

My shoulders slumped. I looked toward the back of the arcade, where all I could see was . . . more line. *Sigh.* I began walking . . . and walking . . . and *walking.*

Finally, after passing what felt like every kid in Royal Woods—and more than a few grown-ups—I reached the end of the line, which was way back in the dark corners of the arcade. Nothing here but stained carpet, a broken Skee-Ball machine, and a moldy, half-eaten doughnut.

My walkie screeched. "Lincoln, how's it going? Have you beaten the high score yet? Is it everything we ever dreamed it would be? Report! Over."

I slumped against the window. "Bad news, Clyde. Operation Outmaneuver My Sisters and Get to the Arcade Before a Giant Line Forms and Also Think of a Shorter Name for This Operation is a bust."

"Noooo!" Clyde's staticky wail pierced my ears, and a few kids looked back at me, still scowling. "Lincoln, what happened? You had it all in the palm of your hand. Did you lose Captain Coinbottom? Did you get squashed by a Martian first thing, in spite of our countless hours of training and simulation? Did you spill a Super Slurp on the game and cause an electrical fire?"

I slid to the ground in a defeated heap. "No, Clyde. It's much worse."

A gasp crackled over the airwaves. "You don't mean . . ."

I nodded glumly, though I knew he couldn't see me. "I didn't beat them, Clyde. Every kid with a pulse is here." I kicked at the ground, adding bitterly, "And even some random grown-ups. Over."

"Oh, Lincoln. What if, somewhere in those hordes, is a video game sensei? A kid able to master every video game he—or she—comes across, with no training or practice, and he—or she—will probably never lose, and will be on it all day, until the sun goes down, and the arcade closes and you'll have to go home with poor Captain Coinbottom, his butt still full of quarters—"

"*Okay,* Clyde, I get it." Sheesh. Operation Be Cheered Up and Cheered On by My Best Friend was also a bust. "I gotta go. I'll update you when I can. Over." I twisted the knob and turned off my walkie.

Knowing I'd be waiting in line for a while, and being the last one in it, I went ahead and busted open Captain Coinbottom at the snack hut and bought an ice-cold Radioactive Berry Super Slurp. I took the long way around back to the end of the line. I didn't want those kids to think I was trying to cut again.

The line had barely moved. I sighed and made a game of drinking my Super Slurp: for every step forward, I took two slurps. Each time the kid in front of me shifted his weight from one foot to the other, I took three slurps. It was a slow game, and pretty dumb, but I had nothing else to do.

Finally, I slurped the last of my drink, wondering, as I always did, how I had managed to empty that much liquid into my belly. I stuck my tongue out as far as I could to see how blue it was. *Huh. The blue of Shiningest Ice Fire, wreaking ultimate Marshmallow Martian destruction! Not bad.*

Still the line barely moved.

A fist-sized yawn was threatening to swallow my face when a familiar voice piped up from behind me.

"Hey, Lincoln."

I turned to find my friend Rusty standing there. His curly orange hair looked extra wild today, as if he'd been jolted by a shock of electricity. Or maybe he was just really excited.

"Hey, Rusty!" I eyed the pockets of his sweatshirt, lumpy with what looked like coins. "I guess you've been saving your allowance, too, huh?"

"Yeah." He crossed his arms, and the money in his pockets jangled. "I've heard about *Marshmallow Martian Blasters* my whole life. My uncle brags about how he always had the highest score and got to Level Inferno as a ten-year-old. So there's this family legacy I have to keep up, or whatever." He sounded glum. Family expectations can be tough.

"Well, did he give you lots of tips for how

to get the most Firesticks? Or how to obliterate the Chunky Chow-Pies?" I asked. "I've heard those are the hardest enemies to beat."

Rusty shook his head. "No. He just said to do him proud and not to die." He raked both hands through his hair, looking more stressed than I'd ever seen him. "Do you know how many ways there are to lose all your Firesticks and get sent back to Earth?"

"Uh . . . twelve?"

"Over a hundred! It doesn't even matter what level you're on," Rusty said, *not* using his indoor voice. "I looked them all up. It's terrible, Lincoln. It's almost impossible to get to Level Lava."

Huh. Not exactly comforting.

I craned my neck, trying to catch a glimpse of the front of the line, but all I saw were endless backs to me, and endless kids waiting for their chance to roast some Marshmallow Martians.

I turned back to Rusty. "This is taking forever."

"You know what else takes forever? Trying to blast through the Graham Cracker Wall of Dominion when you need to eat the Sugar Crystal of Wayfaringness to keep from losing your Mountains of Cookie Rubble shield."

I winced. "More helpful wisdom from your uncle?"

"Yeah. He also said to watch out for the Ptaffy Pterodactyls that swoop in just as you're about to enter the Cave of Smoldering Honeycomb."

"Pterodactyls?" I made a face. "There aren't any pterodactyls on Mars."

"Oh, Lincoln." He sighed as he put a hand

on my shoulder. "You have no idea what's coming, do you? Let me help you."

He slung his arm over my shoulders and told me every terrible way I could lose—my powers, my status, my weapons, my *hair*.

"Okay, *enough*! Sheesh!" Did he think he was helping? This was just making me more nervous, and being nervous always made me have to pee. "Look, Rusty, we're getting close to the front, only seven more kids. Will you hold my spot so I can go pee?"

I was already forming the word *thanks* when Rusty stopped me by shaking his head.

"I can't."

I screeched to a halt, just barely outside the line. "You *can't*?"

"Sorry, Lincoln, but I have to think strategically. I'm on a mission."

"Uh . . . what does me peeing have to do with your mission?" I crossed my arms, and then my legs, too.

"Look, my uncle is counting on me. I have to 'keep the family name unsullied.'"

Un-*what*? "What does that even mean?"

Rusty shrugged. "I don't know. That's just what he said. But I know if I go home and I haven't made it to at least Level Campfire, he'll never be seen in public with me again."

I twisted my legs together harder; the pee rang in my ears, almost blotting out the sounds of the arcade. "Okay, fine, you have to beat the game, but I still don't understand why you can't hold my spot while I pee."

Rusty flipped up the hood of his sweatshirt and pulled it low over his forehead, suddenly menacing. "You're the competition, Lincoln.

And if listening to my *champion* uncle all these years has taught me anything, it's that you *never* help the competition." He leaned closer, staring at me through the shadows from his hood. "You have to pee so bad your eyes are crossing, and that means you won't be able to play well. Or long." He shrugged.

"Rusty, come on. We're buddies," I said.

"There are no buddies on Mars, *buddy*." He looked almost scary.

I jumped back. "Okay, okay, forget I asked. I'll just wait." I turned my back to him, facing the front of the line. Closing my eyes, I tried to count to a hundred Mississippis, but that had the word *pee* in it, and I almost lost it.

Glug, glug, glug.

There was a waterfall behind me. I could hear the water pouring, swishing, flowing. . . .

I crouched into a goblin squat, but I was a dam about to burst. I was dissolving into a rushing torrent. I *was* the waterfall—

Wait. There was a *waterfall* behind me?

I spun around. Rusty was pouring water from one Super Slurp cup to another, back and forth, *glug, glug, glug.*

"Rusty, what are you doing?"

"Sorry, Lincoln, is this bothering you?" He continued to pour long arcs of water from one cup to the other, some of it spilling over the edge and splashing on the ground.

I couldn't take it another second. I was going to explode. Forgetting about the line, the game, and my mission to get the highest score, I raced blindly through the arcade to the restrooms.

When I got to the bathroom, all I found was . . . another line. I clutched my head and tugged sharply on my hair, the slight pain distracting me for a brief second from the fact that I was about to combust.

"Hurry up, hurry up, hurry *uuuuup!*" I squealed. How could there be this many kids needing to pee all at the same time? I bit down on the sleeve of my shirt, but I knew I couldn't make it that long. The pressure was too great.

Just then, the janitor wheeled his mop and bucket by, grumbling about kids and sugar and "too much stimulation" leading to "accidents."

Accidents is right. I was about to have one right now—and that reminded me of the time I'd brought my younger sisters here and Lily had had a diaper "accident." I ended up having to clean her up in the janitor's closet because it was the only place with a big enough sink.

Wait.

The janitor's closet was a tiny hole in the wall, full of rags and cleaning supplies, but it had a giant sink . . . and a TOILET!

Quickly, I looked around to see where he'd gone. *Oh, good.* I saw him by the front door, mopping up what looked like barf. That mess would keep him busy long enough. I hoped.

Trying to be casual in spite of my I-need-to-pee limp, I headed for the hallway where kids weren't supposed to go and found the closet just where I remembered it.

Glancing quickly around to make sure no one could see me, I tried the door. I'm not ashamed to admit a tear sprang to my eye when it opened easily. Slipping inside, I popped the lock and tested it to make sure I'd have privacy. This moment was too important to be worried about interruptions.

The smell of bleach hit me like a fist, but it smelled as good as pizza to me, because there, up against a dingy wall, next to a pile of cleaning rags, was the second most beautiful thing I'd seen all day: an unoccupied toilet.

It was a throne, and I was its king as I . . . well, you get the idea.

Pretty soon the world began to sound normal again. Video games bleeped and pinged, kids laughed; I even heard birds chirping through the window. I sighed happily. I was no longer made of 110 percent water.

I washed up, humming as I used Clyde's bandana to dry my hands. I felt as if I could take on that line again—this time *without* a Super Slurp. Grabbing Captain Coinbottom, I went to unlock the door—only to find that it was stuck.

No.

I tried again, twisting and yanking the knob all the way around, but nothing happened. It wouldn't budge.

I was stuck in the janitor's closet.

I was *stuck* in the *janitor's closet*???

"Help!" I cried as I pounded on the door. "Somebody let me out! I'm stuck in the janitor's closet!"

All I heard were bleeps and pings and kids laughing.

And birds chirping. Laughing at me.

I doubled my efforts, pounding and yelling until my fists were sore.

I was trapped.

And the birds were laughing at me.

Or . . .

Maybe they were *helping* me.

I leapt over to the window I hadn't really paid attention to before and threw it open. The birds scattered, but I didn't care. They had done their part. They got me to the window.

A window that opened onto an alley.

With the ground just five feet below.

I waved at the departing birds. "You can laugh at me anytime you want!"

And the birds started chirping again.

I dropped down into the alley and high-fived myself. I was free!

But I had to get back inside the arcade.

The alley ended to my right but stretched out to my left, all brick walls and trash. And smells. Bad smells.

I pulled my shirt up over my nose and

walked to a door that said NO ENTRY above it. I tugged on the handle anyway, but the sign was right. I couldn't get in.

I tried to breathe through my mouth and scanned the alley again. How was I going to get back into the arcade? Just a few feet away, a narrower alley opened off next to the building and ran to the front, but it was blocked off by a gate too tall to climb.

Dang it.

Then I spied a metal door in the next building with a cartoonish pizza painted on it. Pizza Pirates!

I ran over and tugged on the handle—and it opened! Breathing a sigh of relief, I slipped inside and gave my eyes a minute to adjust to the semidarkness.

After a few seconds I could make out

three doorways, one on either side of me and one straight ahead, at the end of the hallway. Kitchen sounds came from the one on the right—pots and pans banging, water running, people yelling. I peeked inside—lots of people, lots of chaos. I slowly let it shut and moved on to the next door.

Behind the next door were chaos and even more people. Kids and families eating and playing games—including my sisters! I quickly stepped into the shadows, cursing my white hair and bright orange shirt. How was I going to sneak through there without them seeing me? I'm not really known for blending in.

I walked to the end of the hall and inched open the third door. More chaos—this time, shrieking girls around Lisa's age. A birthday cake sat on one of the tables, half eaten, with balloons and presents piled up on another.

But the interesting thing about these girls—besides their lung capacity, *wow;* my ears were ringing—was their faces. Each of them was smeared with paint, much like Lucy's, though there were no skulls here. It was just a bunch of cats and unicorns and what looked like maybe sloths?

Which gave me an idea . . .

Pushing the door open, I stepped in and yelled, "Happy birthday!"

The shrieking stopped as if I'd snuffed out a candle. Instantly all eyes were on me, and then:

"A boy!"

"Who invited a *boy?*"

"Look at his white hair!"

More shrieking.

I rubbed my hair self-consciously but tried

to smile reassuringly. "Whose birthday is it?"

A girl with eyes as big as Lisa's popped up in front of me, orange and black tiger stripes on her face. "Mine! I'm Karla. I'm five!" She held up five fingers.

That must have been some kind of kid-signal, because immediately I was surrounded by at least a dozen five-year-olds shouting their names at me and holding up fingers.

But Karla was the loudest. "Hey, I know you. You go to school with my brother Jimmy."

"Jimmy Lee?"

She smiled and nodded. "I'm Karla Lee!"

"Nice to meet you. I'm Lincoln Loud."

"Lincoln *Loud*!" she shrieked again, followed by a squeal of laughter. "Your last name is *Loud*!"

Another signal, as all the other girls instantly

took up the chorus until my name bounced off the ceiling and I had to stop myself from covering my ears.

I knelt down in front of Karla, and she stopped shrieking. "Hey, can I ask you a favor?"

She nodded, her eyes round and curious.

I pointed at her face. "I see you've got some nice tiger stripes there. Lookin' fierce."

She beamed.

"Do you have any more paint? Say, maybe brown?" I pointed to my hair. "See how white it is? Do you think your paint could color it all brown?"

She jumped and clapped her hands. "Yes, yes, yes! We'll paint your hair!"

"Wait, I didn't mean *you*—"

But she grabbed my hand and dragged me over to a table, forcing me into a chair so small my knees were shoved into my chin.

What felt like a million tiny hands pushed and pulled me this way and that, forcing my chin up, down, and sideways as the girls gleefully argued about whether I should be a sparkly unicorn or a spiky dinosaur or—

"No! Not a sparkly dinosaur—I mean, unicorn—*no green*!" I yelled, but tiny hands clamped over my mouth.

"Hush, Lincoln Loud. We're making you the most magical sparkling merman *ever*."

A merman? I asked for *brown*! How could I sneak by anyone if I was a sparkly merman?

I tried to break free, but those tiny hands were made of steel. How were they so *strong*?

Fingers crawled through my hair like worms. Something wet dripped past my ear. I needed a mirror. I had to know what they were doing.

"Mm-hrrrrmph," I mumbled, trying to force words through the hands over my mouth. But they just clamped down harder.

"Lincoln Loud, stop being so wiggly! Don't you want to look *magical?*"

"Mmff." *No!*

"Let him go." A low, barely audible voice fell on all the giggling like rain. Immediately everyone froze.

I tried to raise my head to see who it was, but the hands held me down.

"I said, *let him go.*"

For a moment it was very, very quiet. Then slowly, the tiny hands let go of me and all the girls stepped back, their eyes wide.

I sprang to my feet, shaking out my arms.

It was good to be my own man again.

Framed in the doorway, still wearing a skull face, stood Lucy.

I glanced back at the party girls. They were bunched together, their eyes big and their hands clenched. Apparently Lucy was scary.

And, even more apparently, I was not.

Sigh.

I hurried over to Lucy. "Thanks. You saved me."

"I know." She looked past me as the party girls resumed their shrieking. "You're up to something, Lincoln."

"I'm not!" I felt bad lying again, but I was too close to completing my mission. I couldn't compromise it now when I was so close to the sweet smell of victory!

"Then why are you being so weird?"

"It's for Clyde," I said, mentally slapping myself as the lies kept piling up. "I didn't want to make a big deal about it, since I kind of took off early, but I extended Project Day to include him, and now I'm helping him with a project. A Clyde project." I held my breath. Would she rat me out? I couldn't read her expression through all that makeup.

"A Clyde project," she said.

I nodded. "A *secret* Clyde project."

"Secret. Uh-huh." She sighed. "Let me guess. Now you want me to help get you out of here without any of our sisters seeing you."

"Yes!" I practically shouted, and was halfway to hugging her before I remembered that Lucy doesn't like outward displays of affection.

I cleared my throat. "If you wouldn't mind."

She flicked a glance at my hair. "Okay, but that's not gonna help."

"Wait, what's not gonna help? Is it green? Tell me it's not green," I said, beginning to panic.

She shook her head. "It's not green."

Phew. White hair wasn't the best for sneaking, but it was miles better than green.

Lucy grabbed a napkin from a stack near the door and tossed it to me. "Here—cover your head with this."

"You said it isn't green."

"It's not." She shot a quick glance at my hair again. "It's pink."

Dang it.

I draped the napkin over my head and peeked past Lucy into the dining room.

"Where is everyone?"

She grabbed my hand and pulled me out of the room. "Don't worry. They're all wrapped up in some new game over there." She waved to the right. "Just keep your head down, and I'll get you outside without them noticing."

I ducked my head, watching my feet as she pulled me through all the tables and games.

Once outside, she whipped the napkin off my head and disappeared back inside before I could even thank her.

I shook my head. Strange kid. Tomorrow I would definitely see whether she still needed help sorting things out with Edwin.

Tomorrow.

Right now I had to get back to the arcade.

I hurried to Gus's Games and Grub, pausing only long enough to catch my reflection in the plateglass windows.

I groaned. My hair was very, *very* pink. And tufted out all over my head like little wings. Not cool at *all*.

I tried to flatten the tufts and thought of

how I'd talked Luan out of putting horns in my hair earlier. Seeing as this is how I ended up looking, I felt kind of bad now that I hadn't let her practice on me.

Oh, well. Time to blast some Martians!

The arcade was a jangle of pings, beeps, and music, with cries of victory and howls of defeat. The smell of sugary drinks and melty cheese— ah, forget it. No time to revel. I had to get to my game!

I all but ran to the spot I'd been trying to get to all day. Rounding some kind of car chase game, I skidded to a stop and came face to face with the impossible. *No line!*

No line, no kids playing the game, no interference. Just me and a bunch of Martians waiting to be blasted.

This moment could not taste sweeter. I took

a deep breath and drank it in, then practically skipped the rest of the way to the game.

I unhooked my walkie from my belt and clicked it on. "Clyde, are you there?" My hands might have been shaking a tiny bit. *"Clyde!"*

"I'm here, buddy. What's the report?"

"I made it. For real this time. The pinnacle of all our dreams, everything we've been working so hard for all these weeks. The game. She is mine. Over!"

"Firesticks, that's amazing!" Clyde took some deep breaths. "I need to sit down." Another pause, then: "Tell me *everything.* Over."

"You got it, buddy! I'm about to start." I set the walkie down and reached for Captain Coinbottom, but my hands grabbed . . . nothing.

Wait. . . .

Where was Captain Coinbottom?

He wasn't there.

When had I last seen him?

I didn't have him outside.

He wasn't in the party room.

Or the alley.

Or the—

That was it! I'd left him in the janitor's closet.

I glanced behind me quickly. Still no one in line. Maybe I could dash back to the closet, grab the Captain, and return before anyone else came to play.

I snatched up the walkie and took off. "Hold on, Clyde, slight hitch. Misplaced the funds. Be right back. Over."

In a few seconds I was at the janitor's closet, yanking on the door. Still stuck.

Dang it.

I stepped from the hallway back into the arcade, searching for the janitor. After a second I spotted a mop bucket sitting next to the far wall. Racing over to it, I found the janitor scrubbing at a crusty brown patch on the wall, grumbling under his breath about "sloppy kids."

"Um, excuse me, sir?"

He held up a hand, silencing me, then took a Super Slurp—Nuclear Orange flavor, by the looks of it—and began to pour it in small streams over the crusty brown mess.

"Whoa, what are you doing?" I couldn't help blurting out. He was just making it worse!

"Pipe down for a second and you'll *see* what I'm doing."

I piped down. After a minute the Super Slurp began to bubble, eating away at the gunk beneath it. In a few more seconds it was soft enough for the janitor to wipe it off with a rag.

"Wow," I said, impressed. "That really worked."

The janitor tucked the rag back in his pocket and scowled at me. "That stuff rots your teeth, too." He stood. "Whaddya want, kid?"

"I need to get into your closet, sir, but the door is stuck."

He glared down at me. "Why in tarnation do you need to get in there?"

"I left Captain Coinbottom inside, sir, and I need—"

"Captain *who*?"

"Captain Coinbottom—er, my piggybank,

sir, with all my allowance in it. You see, I've been—"

He leaned forward and stuck his face in mine. "What's your piggybank doing in my closet?"

"I—uh—had to use the bathroom, sir, and the line was really long, so I thought I'd—"

"You peed in my closet?"

"No—I mean, yes—I mean, I peed in the *toilet* in your closet—"

Without another look at me he stormed off, leaving me and his mop bucket behind. I raced after him.

When we reached the closet, he knelt in front of the door and pressed his ear against it, then slowly twisted the handle with one hand while tapping a line up and down the door with the other. I held my breath.

Then, with startling swiftness, he pounded on the door and yanked the handle at the same time, letting out a mighty bellow. I jumped back.

But—nothing. The door was still stuck.

"Ah, well, I tried." He shrugged and started to walk away.

I grabbed his arm. "You can't just give up! Don't you need your things? Like . . ." I fumbled, trying to remember what I'd seen in the closet earlier. "Bleach?"

He shook me off. "Never said I was giving up, did I? I'm coming back."

Phew. I paced the narrow hallway, unable to keep still. I was *so close.* The moment I'd been fighting for almost as soon as I'd woken up that morning.

Looking back, it seemed as if everyone I'd

run into had been fighting *against* me.

Not. Cool.

Finally, the janitor came back, carrying a chair. Without a glance in my direction he popped it open, settled himself on it, leaned back against the wall, and pulled his cap down over his eyes.

"Um . . . ," I said.

He grunted—or was it a snore?

"Excuse me, sir?"

No reaction.

I leaned forward to tap him on the shoulder, then thought better of it and knocked on the door instead. "Sir?"

"Eh?" He lifted his hat an inch to glare at me. "What is it?"

"I just thought you were going to . . ."

I motioned to the door. "Get it open."

"What does it look like I'm doing?" he asked, settling back against the wall, the cap covering his eyes once again.

Umm . . .

"It looks like you're sleeping. Sir." I tried to keep my tone respectful.

Shoving his cap all the way back, he dropped the chair to all fours and leaned forward, his hands on his knees. "Listen, kid. You ever had a problem you need to solve? You ever had to use your brain and figure out how to solve it? It requires *concentration*. And *imagination*. It's called *creative problem solving*." He leaned back and pulled his cap low again. "I'm working on your problem *right now*."

Wow. That was the kind of reasoning that

would never fly with my parents or teachers. And he was a grown-up!

"It'll go faster if you stop staring at me and run along."

What choice did I have? I ran along.

15

The next hour was miserable. I tried to beg quarters off strangers and even crawled around on the carpet, checking behind and under every game, hoping to find some stray coins, but nope. Nothing.

The long line for *Marshmallow Blasters* had re-formed, and I waited in it three times, hoping each time that when I got to the front, the janitor would show up with Captain Coinbottom.

He didn't.

I watched player after player get higher and higher scores (not to mention lose horribly. Rusty was right. There really were a lot of ways to fail at this game).

And all the while I saw my sisters through the window across the alleyway, having a blast at Pizza Pirates.

This was not how today was supposed to go.

Just as I got in line again, my walkie crackled. "Firesticks? You never reported back. Do you have the top score? Did you get to Level Comet Fire? Is the entire Marshmallow Martian Army reduced to a sticky mess?"

I sighed and clicked my walkie on. "Negative,

Puffmaster. Operation has been compromised."
Badly.

"Again?"

"Yep. Operation Outmaneuver My Sisters and Get to the Arcade Before a Giant Line Forms became Operation Get Someone to Save My Place in Line So I Could Go to the Bathroom became Operation Find a Shorter Line for the Bathroom became Operation Find a Way Out of the Janitor's Closet became Operation Find a Way Through the Alley became Operation Sneak Through Pizza Pirates Without Letting My Sisters See Me became Operation Find My Missing Piggybank became Operation Try to Find Another Way to Play became . . . Operation Watch Everyone Else Play the Game I've Been Waiting Months to Play. Which, ironically, is actually a go."

"*Buddy.* That's crushing. I'm sorry."

I wanted to stop thinking about my utter failure, so I changed the subject. "How did your Operation go?"

"You mean Operation Sacrifice My Saturday to Help My Dads? It went great. They really couldn't have found the last geocache without me. I'm the best at reading coordinates."

I smiled, wondering why I suddenly felt like a heel. "That's great, Clyde. Well, I guess I'll just go home. Operation Know When to Accept Defeat."

"Roger that, buddy. Over."

I sighed and clicked off. I had messed this day up *bad*.

"Hey, kid!"

I looked up to see the janitor standing in front of me, holding out Captain Coinbottom.

"This what you were bellyaching about?"

I gasped and grabbed it from him, hugging it to my chest. "Yes! Thank you, thank you, *thank* you! How'd you do it?"

He leaned closer and dropped his voice. "I *told* you. *Creative problem solving.*" He took a big swig of a Super Slurp and gave me a wink. Then he straightened, and his frown reappeared. "And stay outta my closet."

"Yes, sir! Thanks again!"

He walked off, and the kid who was playing in front of me got sucked into Space Dust Quicksand, another horrible way to die. It was my turn! And I had money!

I couldn't believe the moment was actually

here. My hands were shaking so hard as I slid my quarters into the machine that one fell and rolled away.

I chased it as if my life depended on it, even though I had dozens more in my piggybank. But I couldn't lose one precious shot at beating this game!

The quarter had rolled right up to the window. I snatched it and started to turn around, but something caught my eye.

It was Lucy. She was wrestling with the controller for the claw machine. I saw instantly what she was aiming for: a large goth teddy bear, dressed in stripes and a black beanie, the only dark spot in a sea of pink and blue tutu-wearing, *non*-goth bears.

A gift for Edwin.

But she wasn't going to get it, not with the

way she was handling that claw. It takes a very delicate touch—you have to know just where to position it, and how low to go before releasing the claw. It isn't a skill you can pick up just anywhere. It has to be honed, with hours and hours (and many allowances) of practice, of trying and failing, before you can call yourself an expert (and even then, it *still* takes most of your allowance to get what you were after).

Lucy was no expert . . . but I was.

I looked at Captain Coinbottom. He didn't have sisters, but if he did, I bet he'd help them when they asked him to. He looked like the kind of captain who'd put aside his own plans to be a good brother. He wouldn't pretend he didn't know how to change a diaper.

Or walk in heels.

Or what a proper name for tadpoles is.

Or make up a fake game simply to exhaust and frustrate his sisters.

Or try to blow a contest.

Or make clown make-up depressing instead of amusing.

Or send one sister off by herself instead of just having fun with her.

Captain Coinbottom seemed to stare up at me. Judging.

"Okay, okay, sheesh. You're right, I've been a terrible brother. I sabotaged my family for a video game."

I looked at the quarter in my palm and felt the weight of all my allowances, all my hard work and sacrifices, in my other hand.

All for a video game.

I glanced back at *Marshmallow Martian Blasters,* my quarters already in its belly, waiting for me to come get the high score.

I looked at Lucy, still struggling. Her technique was all wrong. She was just *throwing* her money away.

Video games versus family?

Pffft. No contest.

Family. Every time. Hands down.

I flipped the quarter in the air and caught it, grinning across at Lucy, who had no idea what was coming.

"Hold on, little sister. I'm on my way."

Pizza Pirates was just as loud as the arcade, but somehow my sister managed to make her voice heard over all of it.

"Lincoln!" Lori shouted my name across the room. Instantly every one of my sisters stopped what she was doing and looked around for me.

I waved at them. "Hey, guys!" Then I made

a beeline for Lucy and the claw machine.

Lucy watched me approach. "Lincoln? What are you doing here?" She leaned closer and whispered, "Did you help Clyde with his project?"

I shook my head. "No, but that's not important." By now the rest of my siblings had gathered around me, so I raised my voice and faced them all. "I owe you guys an apology. I wasn't a very helpful Floater this morning."

"See? I *told* you he was being up-to-something weird." Lola looked very satisfied with herself. Then she frowned. "Um, Lincoln, why is your hair pink?"

"Long story." I hung my head. "But you're right. I wasn't being very helpful because all I wanted was to get to the arcade and play this new game that just arrived, *Marshmallow Martian*

Blasters. I've been saving up my allowance for weeks."

"So you purposely messed up as Floater so you could sneak off and play a video game?" Lori's tone was scathing.

"I know. I'm sorry. It was awful of me. I've been a terrible brother. But I'd like to try to make up for it now—at least, to *one* of you. Since the rest of you already finished your projects." I motioned to Lucy to step aside. "Would you allow me? I'm something of an expert."

Lucy moved out of the way. "Okay, but I don't have any more money."

"Don't worry." I held up Captain Coinbottom. "I've come prepared."

Lucy's mouth dropped open. "You're spending your allowance on *me*?"

I shook my head. "I'm spending it on

Operation Win a Goth Bear for My Sister and Try to Be a Better Brother." I popped off Captain Coinbottom's bottom and pulled out a handful of quarters. "Let's do this!"

All my sisters crowded around me as the claw dropped for the first time. Dropped, and missed. They groaned, but I wasn't fazed. I was just getting started.

Quarter after quarter bought me chance after chance, and with each try I got closer. My sisters stayed with me, cheering me on when I got close to snagging the goth bear, groaning when he slipped from the claw's clutches, and laughing in between.

It felt good to be there with all of them, working *for* them instead of against them. I may have messed things up earlier, but here was one thing only I could do—and do well!

Finally, as I was down to my last quarter, I hit my stride and the claw became like putty in my hands. It swayed hypnotically as I maneuvered it into place, then fell like a shot, landing right on top of the goth bear.

"Easy . . . there we go . . . nice and slow . . ." The claw wavered for a moment, acting as if it wasn't going to close, then all of a sudden snapped shut around the bear. I held my breath as it began to lift the bear from the pile. I peered underneath to see if— *Yes!* Its arms overlapped each other underneath the bear, which meant its hold was secure. I had won!

We all watched as the claw swung the bear over to the chute, opening with a satisfying click and dropping the goth bear down so it could slide out into Lucy's waiting hands.

She smoothed his striped bear sweater.

"I'll call him . . . Percival."

Percival? "Hey, that was one of my tadpole names!"

"Ugh, that's a *terrible* name." Lana looked disgusted, then caught a glimpse of Lucy's face. "I mean, it's a terrible name for a tadpole, but *perfect* for a bear wearing eyeliner." She leaned over and whispered to me. "Bears are uppity, too."

Lucy ignored her and nodded at me. "I think Edwin will like him. He gets lonely with me gone at school all day."

I grinned. "What guy doesn't want a pet bear?"

"That was *beary* sweet of you, Lincoln," Luan said, eyes bright. "*Goth* me all choked up."

Lynn whooped. "Loud family high five!"

Everyone surged together and started high-fiving. It was a noisy, *loud* mess—and I couldn't be happier to be a part of it.

Instead of high-fiving me, Lori reached out and tousled my hair—then wiped her hand, which now had a pink smear on it, across my cheek. She leaned over and whispered, "What you did for Lucy was pretty great. You're forgiven, little brother."

I grinned and gave her one heck of a high five.

In the midst of all the hand-slapping, Lisa stepped outside the chaos and cocked her head. "Lincoln, this game you wanted to play—does it have giant puffy green Martians? And blasters that shoot purple candy lasers?"

I stopped and cocked *my* head, looking at her. How did she know? "Yeah . . ."

"Is it that game right there?" She pointed, and I followed her finger to see—

Marshmallow Martian Blasters! Here. At Pizza Pirates. Where I would have been all day if I had just helped my sisters.

Dang it.

Suddenly, all my sisters crowded around me and practically carried me to the game.

"Play it!"

"Here's a quarter!"

"Here's another one!"

"C'mon, little brother, let's see how it's done!"

"Yeah, get the high score! We know you can do it!"

In a blink I found myself standing in front of the game I'd been trying to play all day, joystick in my hand, READY PLAYER ONE flashing.

I couldn't believe it was real. I was actually, *finally* going to blast Martians and sizzle them like bacon and get to Level Sparklers and—

Aaaand I lost. A giant lollipop to the head.

And again. A Chocolate Chow Hound kicked me into outer space.

But wait, this time I had it—nope, lost again. A pair of giant graham crackers with long tentacle arms squished me into a Lincoln Loud sandwich.

In less than ten seconds, I lost all my lives.

DANG IT.